THEO. LESIEG and Dr. Seuss have led almost mystically parallel lives. Born at the same time in Springfield, Mass., they attended Dartmouth, Oxford and the Sorbonne together, and, in the army, served overseas in the same division. When Mr. LeSieg, inevitably, decided to write a children's book, he was, happily, able to prevail on his old friend Dr. Seuss to help him find a publisher. Since then his stories have delighted millions of children around the world.

GEORGE BOOTH, whose drawings appear in many places (but most often in *The New Yorker*), has emerged as one of America's most admired and original cartoonists. Born in Cainsville, Mo., Mr. Booth got his start in the Marine Corps drawing funny pictures for *The Leatherneck*. He was Art Director with Bill Communications, Inc. for several years, then he threw a fit and returned to cartooning. We're glad he did.

Mr. Booth, his wife and daughter live in Stony Brook, N.Y.

Wacky Wednesday was gone
when I counted them all.
And I even got rid
of that shoe on the wall.

"Just find them
and then
you can go
back to bed."

"Only twenty things more
will be wacky," he said.

"Don't be sorry," he smiled.

"It's that kind of a day.

But be glad!

Wacky Wednesday

will soon go away!"

"I'm sorry, Patrolman."
That's all I could say.

I ran
and knocked over
Patrolman McGann.

Then . . .
twelve WORSE things!
I got scared.
And I ran.

Then I
counted
ELEVEN!

I went out

the school door.

Things were worse than before.

I couldn't believe it.

Ten wacky things more!

"Nothing is wacky
here in my class!
Get out!
You're the wacky one!
OUT!"
said Miss Bass.

. . . "Look!
Nine things
are wacky
right here
in your class!"

I ran into school.

I yelled to Miss Bass . . .

"Nothing is wrong,"
they said.
"Don't be a fool."

"But look!" I yelled.
"Eight things are wrong
here at school."

They said,
"Nothing is wacky
around here but you!"

And the Sutherland sisters!
They looked wacky, too.

And then seven more!

I was late for school.

I started along.

And I saw that

six more things were wrong.

I looked
in the kitchen.
I said,
"By cracky!
Five more things
are very wacky!"

I began to dress.
Then I said,
"WOW!"

Four MORE things
were wacky now!

In the
bathroom,
FOUR!

In the
bathroom,
MORE!

Three
more things
were wacky today!

I went
down the hall
and I said,
"HEY!"

More things were wacky!
And I saw three.

I looked out
the window.
And I said,
"GEE!"

Then I
looked up.
And I said,
"Oh, MAN!"

And that's how
Wacky Wednesday
began.

It all began
with that shoe on the wall.
A shoe on a wall . . . ?
Shouldn't be there at all!

TM & text © 1974 by Dr. Seuss Enterprises, L.P.
Illustrations copyright © 1974 by Random House, Inc. All rights reserved
under International and Pan-American Copyright Conventions. Published in
the United States by Random House, Inc., New York, and simultaneously in
Canada by Random House of Canada Limited, Toronto.

Library of Congress Cataloging in Publication Data:
Seuss, Dr.   Wacky Wednesday.
SUMMARY: Drawings and verse point out the many things that are wrong
one wacky Wednesday.   "59."
[1. Counting books. 2. Stories in rhyme]   I. Booth, George, illus.   II. Title.
PZ8.3.G276Wac [Fic] 74-5520
ISBN 0-394-82912-3 (trade)   ISBN 0-394-92912-8 (lib. bdg.).

Manufactured in the United States of America.   50

WACKY WEDNESDAY

By Theo. LeSieg
Illustrated by George Booth

BEGINNER BOOKS   A Division of Random House, Inc.

WACKY WEDNESDAY

GEORGE
WASHINGTON

WACKY WEDNESDAY

Children love to play "What's wrong with this picture?"—searching out all the funny mistakes they can find. But suppose you were to wake up and discover that everything was *really* wacky! That's what happens to the baffled young fellow in Theo. LeSieg's hilarious new book. Everywhere he turns he finds that more and more things are wacky—and nobody else seems to notice. But beginning readers will notice. And as they hunt for all the wonderfully silly things that are wrong on each page, they'll also discover that they are reading —all by themselves.

This book comes from the home of
THE CAT IN THE HAT

Beginner Books

For a list of some other Beginner Book titles, see the back endpaper.

Invasive Species Takeover

SCOTT PEARSON

BLACK
RABBIT
BOOKS

BOLT

Bolt is published by Black Rabbit Books
P.O. Box 3263, Mankato, Minnesota, 56002.
www.blackrabbitbooks.com
Copyright © 2017 Black Rabbit Books

Design and Production by Michael Sellner
Photo Research by Rhonda Milbrett

Library of Congress Control Number: 2015954687

HC ISBN: 978-1-68072-015-0   PB ISBN: 978-1-68072-279-6

Printed in the United States at CG Book Printers,
North Mankato, Minnesota, 56003. PO #1793 4/16

Web addresses included in this book were working and appropriate
at the time of publication. The publisher is not responsible for broken
or changed links.

Contents

CHAPTER 1

Invasion of the

The house sat empty all summer.
While the family was gone, a green
monster climbed over everything.
It covered the doors and windows.
It climbed up the stairs. Even after the
family returned, the monster stayed.
It refused to die.

A Deadly Green Vine

The green monster was really a plant called kudzu. Kudzu is a climbing **vine**. This vine grows over anything. Kudzu vines get so heavy they tip over trees.

Kudzu can grow 12 inches (30 centimeters) in just a day!

ROOTS
AND
CROWN

FLOWERS

LEAVES

VINE

Invasive Species

Kudzu is taking over in parts of the United States. But it's not from there. People brought it to the country. Then the vines began to spread to new places. They hurt plants that already lived there. Kudzu is an **invasive species**.

CHAPTER 2

It Seemed Like a

Good Idea

People brought kudzu to the United States from Japan. They used it as a plant in gardens. Its big leaves made it a good shade plant.

Soon, people found other uses for it. Farmers began feeding it to their animals. They also planted it to stop **soil** from blowing away.

Kudzu TIMELINE

Farmers use kudzu
as animal food.
1920s–1930s

1876
People bring
kudzu to the
United States.

It's Everywhere!

Kudzu grew well in the southern United States. In fact, it grew too well. The warm weather helped it spread quickly. Soon, the vines were growing places they weren't wanted.

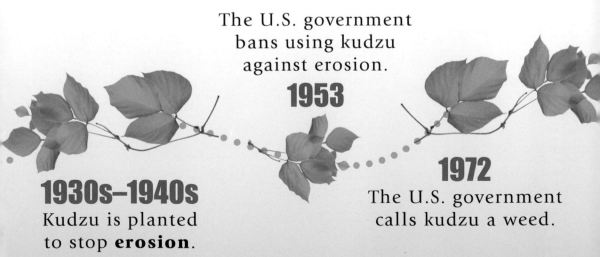

The U.S. government bans using kudzu against erosion.
1953

1930s–1940s
Kudzu is planted to stop **erosion**.

1972
The U.S. government calls kudzu a weed.

KUDZU

Canada

Washington

CHAPTER 3

The Curse of

Kudzu vines grow from a root **crown**. Then, each vine grows roots of its own. So it's very hard to cut down the vines.

These vines cause a lot of problems. Land covered with kudzu can't be farmed. No other plants can grow there. Trees covered with the vine can't be cut. Clearing kudzu away is too hard and costs too much.

Cost of Controlling Kudzu per year

power companies

$1.5 million

farmers and lumber companies

$0

$100 Million

Kudzu Damages Buildings

Kudzu will grow over any building. The vine's roots can crack siding or brick. The vines also hold **moisture** against the walls. This moisture damages buildings too.

Kudzu on railroad tracks makes train wheels slip. The weight of kudzu can also tip over power poles.

$500 million

| $200 Million | $300 Million | $400 Million | $500 Million |

CHAPTER 4

Stopping Kudzu

Getting rid of kudzu is hard. It's much easier to stop it before it overtakes an area. Cutting off the vine's crown kills it. Some people use **chemicals** to kill crowns too.

But the vines grow quickly. If not taken care of, the vines will take over. A space the size of a bedroom can have more than 200 crowns.

crown vetch leaves

poison ivy leaves

Is It
Kudzu?

kudzu leaves

Fungus versus Kudzu

Scientists have found a **fungus** that kills kudzu. During tests, the fungus started working in less than a day. Scientists need to do more testing on this discovery. But it might be a way to stop kudzu.

The fungus doesn't harm other plants.

Look Out for a Takeover!

Kudzu is a troublemaker. But it can be used for some good. People can make jelly from the plant's flowers. The leaves can be eaten like spinach. But without care, the vines will take over. And people will be eating kudzu for supper every day!

KUDZU BY THE NUMBERS

UP TO

100
FEET
(30 meters)

**LENGTH OF
ONE VINE**

**6 to 12
FEET**
(2 to 4 m)

DEPTH OF A ROOT

120,000
ACRES
(48,562 hectares)

**DISTANCE
KUDZU SPREADS
EACH YEAR**

3 TO 10
INCHES
(8 to 25 cm)

LEAF LENGTH

Think about It. . .

1. Chemicals can kill kudzu, but many people don't want to use them. Use other sources to find out why chemicals might not be a good solution.

2. Animals can eat kudzu. Should farmers plant it in order to feed their animals? Explain why or why not.

3. What do you think should be done about the kudzu problem? Use facts to support your answer.

GLOSSARY

chemical (KE-muh-kuhl)—a substance that can cause a change in another substance

crown (KROWN)—the part of a root from which a plant's stem grows

erosion (e-ROW-zhun)—the slow wearing away of something by water or wind

fungus (FUN-gus)—a living thing, similar to a plant that has no flowers, that lives on dead or decaying things

invasive species (in-VAY-siv SPEE-seez)—animals or plants that spread through an area where they are not native, often causing problems for native plants and animals

moisture (MOYS-chur)—a small amount of liquid that makes something wet

soil (SOYL)—the loose surface material of the earth in which plants grow

vine (VIYN)—a plant with very long stems and that grows along the ground or up something

LEARN MORE

Kallio, Jamie. *12 Things to Know about Invasive Species.* Today's News. Mankato, MN: Peterson Pub. Co., 2015.

O'Connor, Karen. *The Threat of Invasive Species.* Animal 911: Environmental Threats. New York: Gareth Stevens Publishing, 2014.

Spilsbury, Richard. *Invasive Plant Species.* Invaders from Earth. New York: PowerKids Press, 2015.

WEBSITES

Invasive Species: Plants–Kudzu
www.invasivespeciesinfo.gov/plants/kudzu.shtml

Kudzu
www.se-eppc.org/manual/kudzu.html

PCA Alien Plant Working Group–Kudzu
www.nps.gov/plants/alien/fact/pumo1.htm